D1580181

C334432981

Alfie's Castle

by Jackie Walter and David Arumi

W
FRANKLIN WATTS
LONDON•SYDNEY

It was Alfie's birthday.

He opened the biggest present.

It was a castle.

Alfie was very happy.

"Thank you," he said.

Dad looked at all the bricks

inside the box.

He picked up a bag

of little white bricks

and tipped them onto the table.

Mum picked up a bag
of little grey bricks
and tipped them onto the carpet.

Grandad picked up a bag

of little brown bricks

and tipped them onto the carpet.

Dad tried to make a castle.

But the little white bricks

did not fit together.

"This doesn't look right," he said.

9

Grandad tried to make a castle.

But the little brown bricks

fell over.

"This doesn't look right," he said.

11

Mum tried to make a castle.

But the little red bricks

did not stand up.

"This doesn't look right," she said.

13

Alfie took a book out of the box.

"Stop!" he said.

"You all need to look at this!"

"Mum, you make the tower.
Dad, you make the walls.
Grandad, you make the gate,"
said Alfie.
"I will help you."

17

Alfie helped Mum make the tower

He helped Dad make the walls.

He helped Grandad make the gate

"Thank you, Alfie," they said.

Story trail

Start

Start at the beginning of the story trail. Ask your child to retell the story in their own words, pointing to each picture in turn to recall the sequence of events.

Independent Reading

This series is designed to provide an opportunity for your child to read on their own. These notes are written for you to help your child choose a book and to read it independently.

In school, your child's teacher will often be using reading books which have been banded to support the process of learning to read. Use the book band colour your child is reading in school to help you make a good choice. *Alfie's Castle* is a good choice for children reading at Blue Band in their classroom to read independently.

The aim of independent reading is to read this book with ease, so that your child enjoys the story and relates it to their own experiences.

About the book

When Alfie gets a brick castle for his birthday he's super excited! All the family try to help build it, but nothing seems to fit together. Then Alfie discovers some instructions ... and the need for teamwork!

Before reading

Help your child to learn how to make good choices by asking: "Why did you choose this book? Why do you think you will enjoy it?" Look at the cover together and ask: "What do you think the story will be about?" Support your child to think of what they already know about the story context. Read the title aloud and ask: "Why do you think Alfie is opening a new toy?" Remind your child that they can try to sound out the letters to make a word if they get stuck.

Decide together whether your child will read the story independently or read it aloud to you. When books are short, as at Blue Band, your child may wish to do both!

During reading

If reading aloud, support your child if they hesitate or ask for help by telling the word. Remind your child of what they know and what they can do independently.

If reading to themselves, remind your child that they can come and ask for your help if stuck.

After reading

Support comprehension by asking your child to tell you about the story. Use the story trail to encourage your child to retell the story in the right sequence, in their own words.

Give your child a chance to respond to the story: "Did you have a favourite part? What did Alfie discover after the pieces didn't fit? Why didn't he spot the problem at the start?"

Help your child think about the messages in the book that go beyond the story and ask: "Why do you think each person had trouble making their part? What does Alfie learn about working with many people at once? Have you ever worked in a team before? What did you learn?"

Extending learning

Help your child understand the story structure by using the same sentence patterns and adding some new elements. "Let's make up a new story. 'Suzy got a toy train set.Dad took the white tracks, Mum took the blue tracks and Grandma took the grey tracks. But the pieces didn't fit.' What will happen in your story?"

In the classroom your child's teacher may be reinforcing punctuation. On a few of the pages, check your child can recognise capital letters, full stops and question marks by asking them to point these out.

Franklin Watts
First published in Great Britain in 2019
by The Watts Publishing Group

Copyright © The Watts Publishing Group 2019

Series Editors: Jackie Hamley and Melanie Palmer
Series Advisors: Dr Sue Bodman and Glen Franklin
Series Designer: Peter Scoulding

A CIP catalogue record for this book is
available from the British Library.

ISBN 978 1 4451 6807 4 (hbk)
ISBN 978 1 4451 6809 8 (pbk)
ISBN 978 1 4451 6808 1 (library ebook)

Printed in China

Franklin Watts
An imprint of
Hachette Children's Group
Part of The Watts Publishing Group
Carmelite House
50 Victoria Embankment
London EC4Y 0DZ

An Hachette UK Company
www.hachette.co.uk

www.franklinwatts.co.uk